# Disney's

# Winnie the Pooh
## and **Valentines, Too**

Liza Alexander

ILLUSTRATED BY Carol Christensen Haantz

DISNEY
PRESS

New York

Printed in the United States of America.

The type for this book was set in 15-point Cochin.

The artwork for each picture was prepared using watercolor and pencil.

Based on the Pooh stories by A. A. Milne (copyright The Pooh Properties Trust).

First Edition
1 3 5 7 9 10 8 6 4 2

Library of Congress Catalog Card Number: 98-85116
ISBN: 0-7868-3217-7

# Winnie the Pooh
## and Valentines, Too

Ⅰn the deep of every winter comes a most delightful event—
Valentine's Day! On this day or thereabouts, Winnie the Pooh
skipped through the Hundred-Acre Wood. As he reached the top of
the Enchanted Hill, a chill wind whistled.

"How rather odd," said the bear. He was think-think-thinking
about his best friend. "Christopher Robin is always here, except for
when he isn't." Pooh smiled. "Which must mean he is elsewhere."

The first place Pooh thought to look was Piglet's, where Piglet tried very hard to hide what he was doing from Pooh. "Maybe Christopher Robin is busy with a surprise . . . maybe not. Depending," said Pooh.

"Depending on what?" Piglet asked.

"Yes, on what," answered Pooh. "And what is that you have there, Piglet?"

Piglet sighed. "I was making a Valentine's card for you."

"Perhaps that is what Christopher Robin is doing," said Pooh.
So Pooh and Piglet gathered their friends and hurried to see what
Christopher Robin was doing.

Pooh, Piglet, Tigger, Gopher, Rabbit, and Eyore found Christopher Robin, without him finding them, and saw that he was writing the letters W-I-N.

"It's your name, Pooh," said Rabbit. "He's spelling W-I-N-the Pooh!"

"Oh-ho!" said Pooh, rather pleased, until Christopher Robin read the words out loud.

"Dear Winifred," he read.

Pooh was confused. "But what, precisely, is a Winnyfred?"

Pooh and his friends knew that this was a question for Owl. So off they went.

"A Winifred," proclaimed Owl, "is a girl. When a boy reaches a certain age, sometimes a girl becomes of interest."

"Does that mean Christopher Robin will no longer be interested in us?" asked Pooh.

"My dear bear!" continued Owl. "This fellow's been bitten by a love-bug! He's suffering from lovesickness."

"Then we must get him to a doctor!" said Pooh.

"Easy, Pooh boy," Tigger said. "We have to get another lovebuggy to *un*bite him! And to catch a bug, you need bait!"

In the Hundred-Acre Wood, Tigger set a trap on top of a hill. The trap was laid with bait, and the bait was Piglet! Tigger bounced about. "What lovable bug could resist this lovely young lad?"

"Isn't that hilltop actually an ant bed?" wondered Pooh.

"Oh, d-d-d-dear!" Piglet cried. He scurried off the anthill.

"Bother," said Pooh. "Something has found my honey."

Tigger and Rabbit took a closer look at the something. "It's the LOVEBUG!" they shouted at once. The bug flew away and disappeared into the forest.

"We must find it," said Pooh, "or Christopher Robin will never again be as he was."

So the friends searched and searched until they found themselves deep in the heart of the forest.

"I do hope these l-lovebugs aren't f-fierce c-creatures," worried Piglet.

"They're monstrous things all right!" warned Gopher. "One bite and . . ."

"You grow into a great lumbering beast, out of control!" continued Rabbit.

"And when the lovebug bites you, you start making all sorts of spooky sounds!" added Tigger. Then he saw it. "After that bug!"

Willy-nilly, each of the friends ran off in a different direction.

Piglet was lost in the dark. "P-p-p-pooh Bear . . . ?" he whispered.

"*P-p-p-pooh Bear?*" the dark echoed back.

Gopher reached to grab on to Piglet's hand. "Don't worry, Piglet old pal, jussst keep a tight hold of—" It was not Piglet's hand. "Aaaaaaaagh!"

Tigger shivered. "Being all by their lonely lonesomes is not something Tiggers like best!"

"Alone in the dark," Eeyore sighed. "Pretty much says it."

"I have it!" yelled Pooh. He caught the lovebug in a jar and
fastened the top. "Now Christopher Robin will be quite all right!"
Then Pooh saw that he was all alone. "If only Christopher Robin
were here to show me the way."

Just then the lovebug started to glow. "Oh my!" said Pooh.
He opened the jar and set the bug free. It showed a path for Pooh
to follow.

And the lovebug
lit Gopher's way . . .

. . . and Rabbit's . . .

. . . and Eeyore's . . .

. . . and the lovebug
showed Piglet his way, too.

"The lovebug brought us out of the dark and back together!" said Rabbit.
Pooh caught the bug in the jar.

"And now we can get it back to Christopher Robin so Christopher Robin
can get back to being Christopher Robin!" said Tigger.

"And then he can get back to being with us!" said Pooh.

As they reached the top of the knoll, Christopher Robin came running. "I've been looking everywhere for you!" he said. "There's something I wanted to show you."

Tigger nudged Pooh. "Go on, buddy bear, let him have it!"

Pooh hid the jar behind his back. Christopher Robin didn't notice. "I made this card for a new friend. And I wonder what you think of it, Pooh."

Pooh put down the jar and took the card. "It's very nice indeed," he said.

Christopher Robin smiled and looked again at the card he'd made for Winifred.

Pooh stepped aside. He opened the jar and set the lovebug free. Christopher Robin didn't notice.

But Rabbit and Tigger did.

And so did Piglet. "Why did you let it go?" he asked.

"Because Christopher Robin is happy as he is, and I shouldn't want it any other way," answered Pooh.

As the day ended, the friends were discouraged. They trudged
back through the Hundred-Acre Wood to their homes.

But the next morning, each friend found a Valentine's Day surprise in his mailbox.

"Hmm, what have we here?" wondered Rabbit.

"Z-X-L-Q-M. Yessiree, that spells Gopher, so it's for me!" said Gopher.

"What's th-this?" stuttered Piglet.

"Well, look at what somebody made for little old me!" Tigger bounced.

"Mistake, no doubt," sighed Eeyore when he saw his card.

Pooh huffed and puffed as he ran up the Enchanted Hill to find Christopher Robin. "It's a card from you! Is it really for me!?"
"It really is," answered Christopher Robin.

"But we thought you found a new friend," said Pooh.

"Oh, Pooh Bear, just because I care about someone else, it doesn't mean I care any less for you."

"Yes. I thought that, too. Still, it's nice to hear it said."

"Silly old bear!" Christopher Robin took Pooh's hand and off they climbed toward the crest of the hill.